Table of contents

A book about culture 4
Parts of a book 6
Culture words to know 8
More culture words 10
Big ideas about culture 12
Plan out your writing 14
Start researching! 16
Body of the book 18
"Sensing" culture 20
Writing or typing? 22
Time to share! 24
Editing and proofreading 26
Designing your book 28
Celebrate your book! 30
Glossary, Index, and Further reading 32

A book about culture

Culture is the way we live. It is the clothes we wear, the foods we eat, the languages we speak, how we dance, make music, and celebrate, and the ways in which we show how creative we are. This book teaches you how to write a **non-fiction** book about culture. A non-fiction book is true. It can contain stories about real people or facts about animals, habitats, countries, history, and, of course, culture. **Fiction** books tell stories created from someone's imagination. The stories did not really happen. Both fiction books and non-fiction books are a part of culture.

Writing a book about culture will make you feel creative. ***Publishing*** *your book will make you feel proud. To publish something is to share it with others. Will you write and publish a book about your culture?*

I can write a book series

I can write a book about Culture

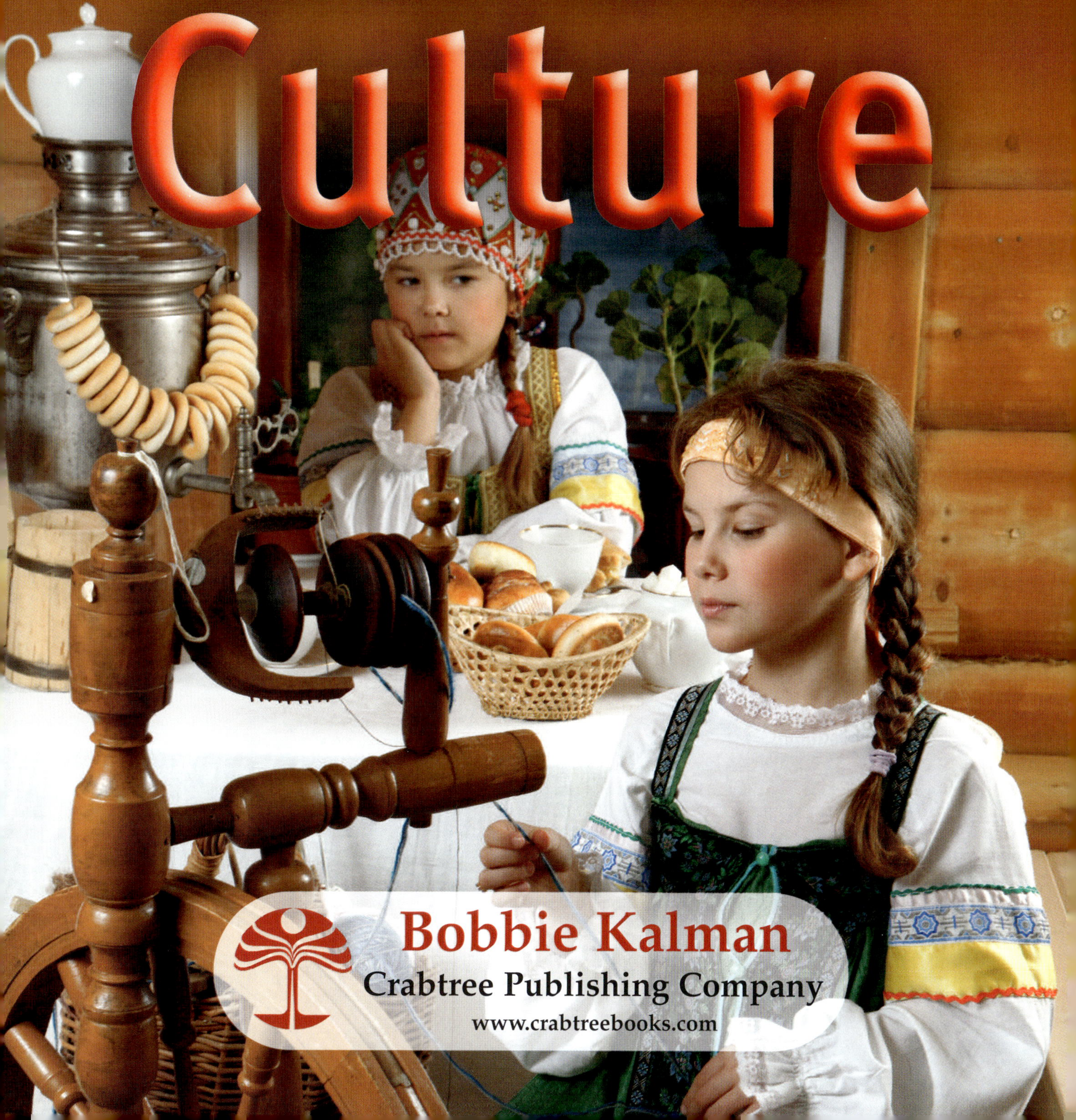

Bobbie Kalman

Crabtree Publishing Company

www.crabtreebooks.com

I can write a book series

Created by Bobbie Kalman

For my new friend Fran Maiolo
I love exploring local culture with you!

Author and Editor-in-Chief
Bobbie Kalman

Editors
Kathy Middleton
Crystal Sikkens

Photo research
Bobbie Kalman

Design
Bobbie Kalman
Katherine Berti
Samantha Crabtree (logo and cover)

Prepress technician
Katherine Berti

Print and production coordinator
Katherine Berti

Photographs
Adobe/Image Club: p. 10 (bottom left)
Katherine Berti: p. 30 (open binder)
Istockphoto: p. 10 (top right)
Bobbie Kalman: back cover inset, p. 5 (box inset), 25 (top right box inset), 29 (top right box inset)
Shutterstock: cover, logo, title page, p. 3, 4, 5 (all except box inset), 6, 8 (top right), 9 (center and bottom), p. 10 (top left and bottom right [except for workshop inset]), 11–17, 19–22, 23 (bottom left and right), 24, 25 (all except top right box inset), 26, 27, 28, 29 (all except top right box inset and top left cover main image), 30 (all except open binder), 31; Sergei Bachlakov: p. 9 (top left); Chen WS: p. 29 (top left cover main image); Patrick Hermans: p. 23 (center left); Jeff Schultes: p. 10 (bottom right [workshop inset]); Stanislaw Tokarski: p. 8 (bottom); Victorian Traditions: p. 8 (top left)

Library and Archives Canada Cataloguing in Publication

Kalman, Bobbie
I can write a book about culture / Bobbie Kalman.

(I can write a book series)
Includes index.
Issued also in electronic format.
ISBN 978-0-7787-7989-6 (bound).--ISBN 978-0-7787-7998-8 (pbk.)

1. Culture--Juvenile literature. 2. Composition (Language arts)--Juvenile literature. 3. English language--Composition and exercises--Juvenile literature. 4. Book design--Juvenile literature. I. Title. II. Series: Kalman, Bobbie. I can write a book.

GN357.K325 2012 j306 C2012-901166-5

Library of Congress Cataloging-in-Publication Data

Kalman, Bobbie.
I can write a book about culture / Bobbie Kalman.
p. cm. -- (I can write a book series)
Includes index.
ISBN 978-0-7787-7989-6 (reinforced library binding : alk. paper) -- ISBN 978-0-7787-7998-8 (pbk. : alk. paper) -- ISBN 978-1-4271-7880-0 (electronic pdf) -- ISBN 978-1-4271-7995-1 (electronic html)
1. Written communication. 2. Communication and culture. 3. Social history. I. Title.

P211.K314 2012
808.06'63--dc23

2012005876

Crabtree Publishing Company
www.crabtreebooks.com 1-800-387-7650

Printed in Canada/042012/KR20120316

Published in Canada
Crabtree Publishing
616 Welland Ave.
St. Catharines, Ontario
L2M 5V6

Published in the United States
Crabtree Publishing
PMB 59051
350 Fifth Avenue, 59th Floor
New York, New York 10118

Published in the United Kingdom
Crabtree Publishing
Maritime House
Basin Road North, Hove
BN41 1WR

Published in Australia
Crabtree Publishing
3 Charles Street
Coburg North
VIC 3058

Learning and teaching

Writing is like an adventure that never ends. The more you know, the more you want to discover. When you discover new things about the world, you want to share your knowledge with everyone! Writing a book allows you to do that. Not only are you an **author**, you are a teacher, too, because your readers learn from you. What will you teach others about culture?

Bobbie's "tweet"

The "rainforest bird" on the left is me, Bobbie Kalman. In this photo, I was at a school talking to some students about the culture of Brazil, in South America. The Amazon rain forest is located there, the home of the beautiful birds you see flying around the picture. Before I became an author, I was a teacher. Since then, I have written more than 800 non-fiction books. Now, I teach through my books. I love writing because I learn new and amazing things every day! The day this photo was taken, the students and I made wonderful music together. We had a lot of fun creating culture.

Parts of a book

Have you written projects or reports for school? Writing a non-fiction book is like writing a report, but there are more parts to a book. The **cover** is the outside of a book. It holds a book's pages together, and it is the first part of a book that people see. When people see an interesting cover, they want to read the book. How will your cover look? Will you have one main picture or several? What do you like about the cover of this book?

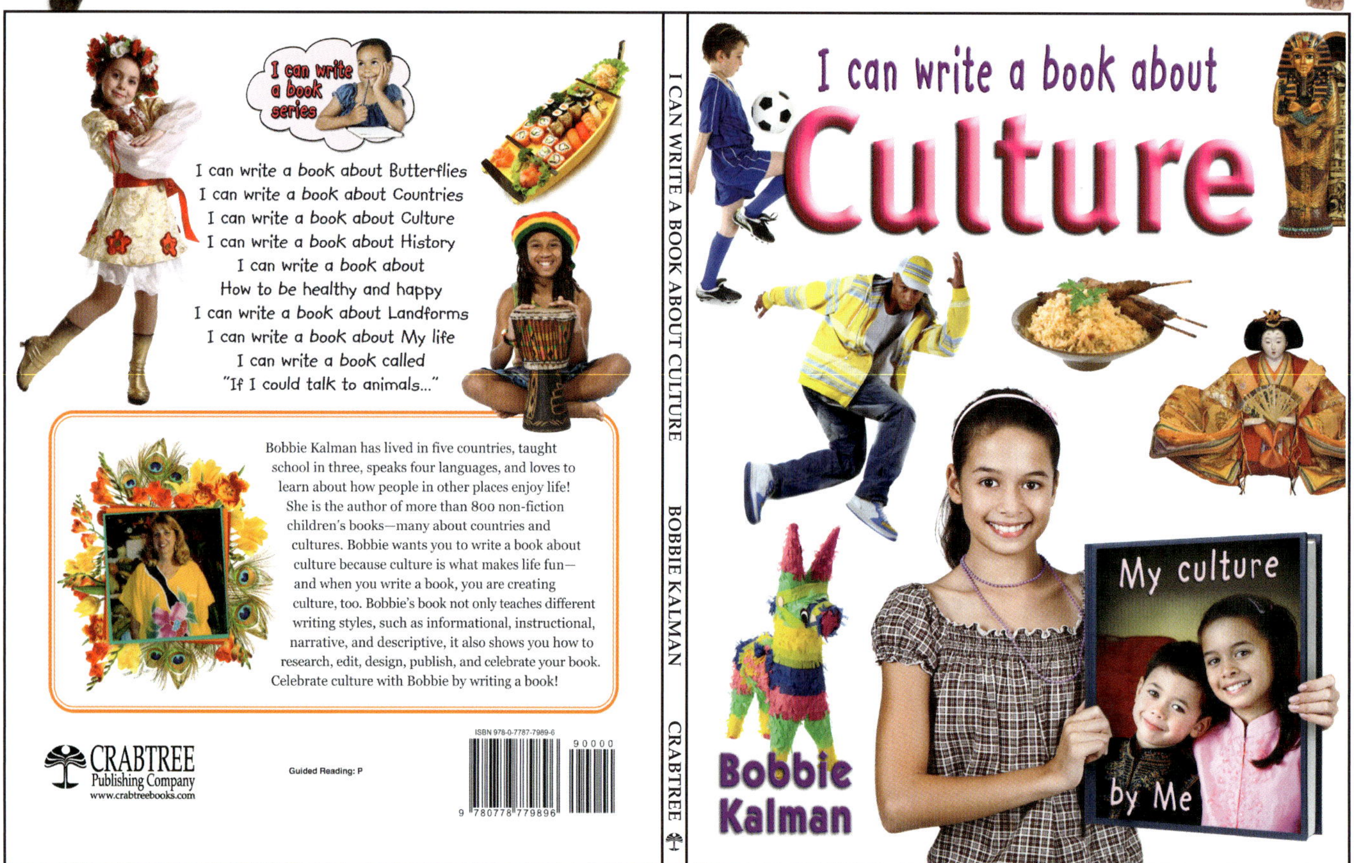

*The back cover of the book may give you information about the author, **publisher**, price, and other books written by the author.*

*The **spine** of the book has the title, author, and publisher's name. It helps you find a book on a bookshelf.*

The front cover of the book contains the title of the book and the name of the author. It catches your attention with an interesting title or a great picture or pictures.

The title page

The first page of a book is the **title page**. The picture on the right shows the title page of this book. What information does it give you?

Copyright page

The second page in this book is the **copyright** page. Copyright means that people cannot copy all or parts of the book without the author's or publisher's permission. What else does it tell you? Turn to the copyright page in this book and find the following information:

- the names of the people who helped create this book
- the addresses of the publisher
- the **dedication** of the book, or the words used to honor someone by placing his or her name in the book
- the **cataloging information**, a section of the page that tells the books's title, the name of the author, the year the book was published, and the type of book it is

Contents, glossary, index

The **table of contents** gives the names of the **chapters**, or sections, in the book and the page numbers on which they begin. The **glossary** is a small dictionary that explains special words used in the book. The **index** is an alphabetical list of the topics in the book with page numbers telling where those topics are covered.

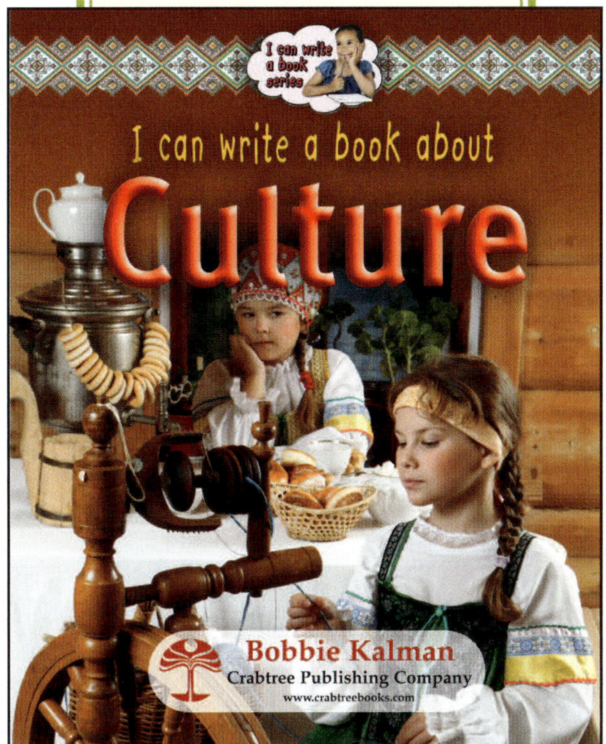
I can write a book series
I can write a book about
Culture
Bobbie Kalman
Crabtree Publishing Company
www.crabtreebooks.com

The top picture shows the title page of this book, and the bottom one shows the table of contents.

Table of contents

A book about culture	4	"Sensing" culture	20
Parts of a book	6	Writing or typing?	22
Culture words to know	8	Time to share!	24
More culture words	10	Editing and proofreading	26
Big ideas about culture	12	Designing your book	28
Plan out your writing	14	Celebrate your book!	30
Start researching!	16	Glossary, Index,	
Body of the book	18	and Further reading	32

Culture words to know

The next four pages introduce you to the most important words about culture. They will help you write your book. Your glossary will be at the end of your book. You can do a picture dictionary with definitions underneath, a glossary without pictures, or both. Learn more about glossaries on pages 31 and 32.

***Ancestors** are people in our families who were alive long before we were. We are their **descendants**, or family members who were born many years later.*

***Art** is a way of using colors, shapes, and textures to create paintings, buildings, or statues. People show their imagination and cultures through art.*

***Carnival** is a week-long party that usually takes place in February in many countries in Europe, South America, and the Caribbean. In some countries, it is called **Mardi Gras**. Music, dancing, and parades with costumes are part of Carnival and Mardi Gras. This girl is part of a carnival parade. She is dressed as a rainforest bird, just as I am on page 5.*

A ***celebration*** is having fun at an event, such as a birthday party, holiday, or special time of the year. A ***festival*** is a time of celebration that often includes costumes, music, dance, and parades, such as this Chinese New Year Festival.

*A **continent** is one of seven huge areas of land on Earth. Write the names of the seven continents on the blackboard or in a notebook.*

__Classical__ describes art, music, or dance that has been done in a certain way for a long time.

*A **country** is an area of land with **borders** and a **government**. A border is an imaginary line that separates countries. A government runs a country.*

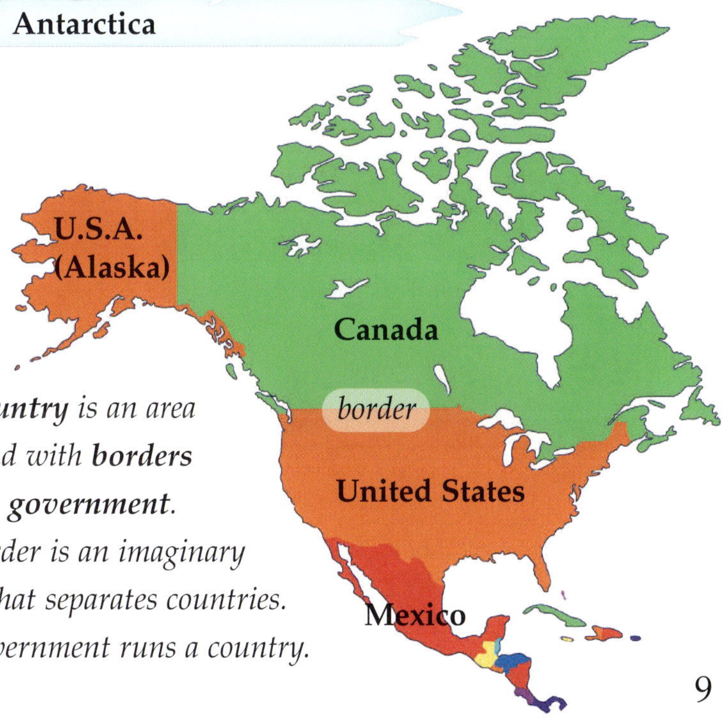

More culture words

A **custom** is a way of doing something that is accepted by a culture, such as giving gifts on someone's birthday.

Diversity is a variety of people and cultures. **Multicultural** means "made up of many cultures." Many countries are multicultural.

History is a record of how people lived in the past. It can be passed down in writing or through spoken stories. The picture above shows pioneers traveling in wagons to the western lands of North America to start new lives.

Historic describes something that is a part of history.

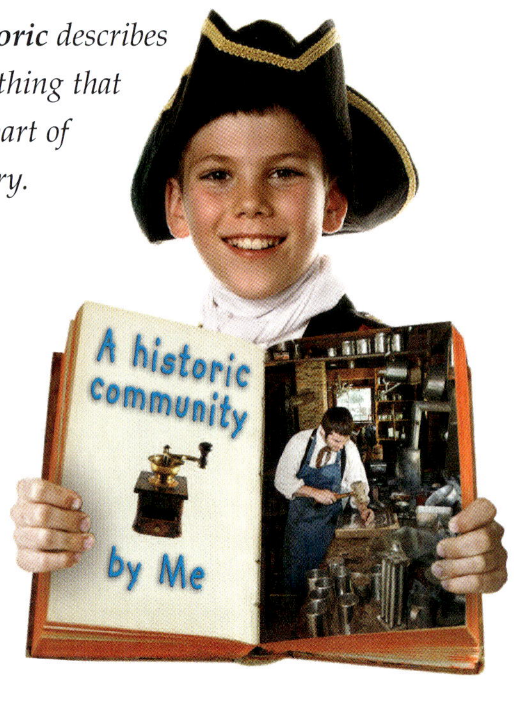

Language *is how people communicate by talking or writing, using words they understand. Many people speak more than one language.*

Immigrants *are people who have left their home countries to come and live in a new country. Are you or any students in your class immigrants?*

A ***pioneer*** *is one of the first people to* ***settle****, or live, in an area. Pioneers lived in villages like this one. You can visit a pioneer village to learn about how people lived 150 years ago.*

Tradition *is a set of beliefs or ways of doing things that are passed down through families or cultural groups. Many people in the United States and Canada celebrate Thanksgiving with a* ***traditional*** *turkey dinner. Traditional describes something that is practiced according to a tradition.*

Big ideas about culture

People live in different countries on all of Earth's continents, except Antarctica. Our ancestors lived in one country, but we may live in another. Our cultures have come partly from our ancestors and partly from how and where we live now. Culture is everywhere and is part of everything we do. These pages show some of the **big ideas**, or important topics, that make up culture. They are history, music and dance, holidays and celebrations, clothing, food, games and sports, and art. What parts of culture do you enjoy? Are you an artist, a dancer, an athlete, or a musician? Your favorite things are what you should write about. When you write a book, you share them with others.

What is your culture?

- What is your family's culture?
- In which country did your ancestors live? Where were you born?
- Are your parents from different countries?
- What traditions do you celebrate?
- Describe the traditional clothing you wear every day or at special times.
- What languages do you or your parents speak?
- Each of the words below means hello. Find out where people use these greetings.

Hello Guten Tag Bonjour Szia
Aloha Shalom
Bongiorno Jambo Ni hao
Hola Privyet Konnichiwa Hej

traditional clothing, art, and language

music

history

What is history?

- Who were the first peoples living in your country?
- Have you visited a historic community in your area?
- How do you celebrate the history or birthday of your country?

traditional dance

Music, dance, celebration

- What kind of music do you listen to?
- Do you play any musical instruments?
- Do you perform any classical or traditional dances?
- What are your favorite celebrations?
- How does your family celebrate them?

holidays and celebrations

Games and sports

- What games or sports do you play?
- Which sports do you like to watch?

sports

The art of culture

- What is your favorite kind of art?
- What kind of art do you create? Do you like to draw, paint, or take photographs?

Tasting culture

- Are there special foods that are part of your family's culture? Do you eat them every day or during certain times of the year?
- Which kinds of foods have you tried? Have your eaten Italian, Chinese, Thai, or foods from other countries?

food

Plan out your writing

Before you start writing, you need to plan what you will write about. Choose a topic or topics that interest you and make you feel excited. Read the questions below and write your answers and thoughts in a "writer's notebook." Use your notebook to record the information you have learned. Keep it handy so you can add new ideas as you think of them.

Ask your teacher if you can work together with some other students. It's fun to work on books with others.

Questions to ask

- What do I know about a culture that I could share with others?
- Which part of a culture do I want to learn more about?
- Do I want to write about my family's culture or learn about other cultures?
- How has cultural diversity made my life more interesting?
- How will I make my book exciting for others to read?
- How will I find information?

Prewriting

- Choose the parts of culture that are interesting to you and learn everything about them.
- Make an outline of the topics you will be writing about. Your outline will become your table of contents.
- Choose some topics from the list below and add your own.

kimono

Hina Matsuri, *also called Girl's Festival, is celebrated by Japanese families. Girls display special dolls and wear traditional kimonos.*

Culture topics

What is culture?
Countries and cultures
Traditional clothing
Music and dance
Favorite foods
Games and sports
Art and history
Changing cultures
Celebrating culture
Important holidays
Our multicultural world
How are we the same and different?
Fun with culture

ballet

The Russian girl above is drinking tea and eating round biscuits during Pancake Week, which celebrates the end of winter.

This girl does not live in Mexico, but she wants to learn about her roots. She is visiting the place where her ancestors once lived.

piñata

maracas

Start researching!

This book introduces you to some important facts about culture, but you will need to **research**, or look for, more facts. Reading the books about culture and celebrations, shown on these two pages, is a great way to start. They may be in your school or public library. You can also find information in other books, encyclopedias, television programs, at cultural centers in your community, and on the Internet. Use at least two sources for your research. Take notes, but be sure not to copy someone else's work word for word. Read and understand the information, then rewrite it in your own words.

Your school library may have all the books you need. If not, you can visit the public library near you, as well.

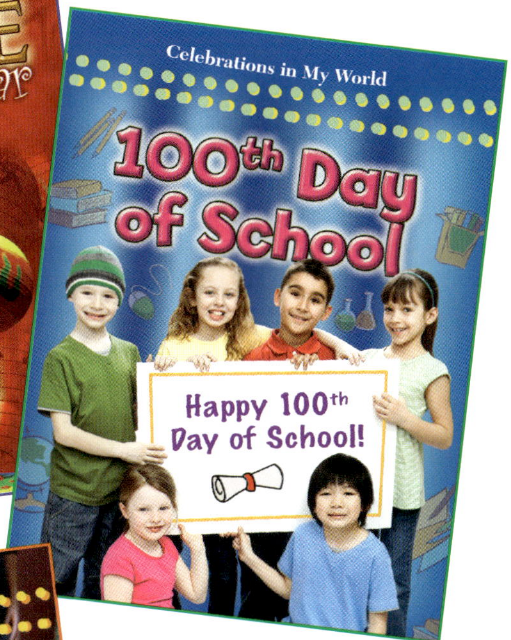

Remember!

- Use at least two research sources.
- Write research information in your own words.
- Interview someone from another culture.
- Include your own experiences, adding photographs of your cultural activities.
- When you paint a picture or write a book, you are creating culture.

There are many other titles that will help you research information for your book. See page 32 for more information on these books.

There are videos on the Internet of people dancing, making music, and celebrating holidays and festivals. Ask your teacher which videos you could watch.

Body of the book

Now that you have done some research, it is time to start writing the **body** of the book. The body of the book contains information, facts, and stories you have learned and will share with others.

Spreads and headings

You will find writing a book easier if you organize your ideas into small chapters called **spreads**. A spread is two pages that face each other. Each spread has a **heading**. A heading tells you what a chapter is about. A spread may have several paragraphs separated by **subheadings**. A subheading is a paragraph heading, which is smaller than the chapter heading. It tells you what a paragraph is about.

Our multicultural world

We live in a **multicultural** world. Multicultural means "made up of many cultures." People are different, but we are also the same. We are the same because we all need air, water, and food. We are the same because we all share the same home. Earth is our home. We are connected to one another because we live on Earth.

26

We are family!

People in a family are alike, but they are not the same. All over this world, people are different, too. We speak different languages, we sing different songs, we have different religions, and we show our imaginations in different ways. We have different talents and dreams. If we were all the same, Earth would be a boring place. The cultures in our world make Earth an exciting and fun place to live!

Diversity means variety.
Variety is colorful and fun.
Fun makes us feel free—
free to be different, you and me,
part of this big Earth family!

You have a whole world of sisters,
and a whole world of brothers, too.
Your Earth family is a wonderful thing.
Does it make you want to sing?

27

The spread above is from the book called What is Culture? *shown at the top of page 16 of this book. What is the heading of the spread? What is the subheading?*

From introduction to ending

The beginning of your book introduces the subject and explains what it is. The middle part of your book provides several spreads of information about the subject. The ending of your book may challenge your reader with interesting ideas or an activity.

Introduce the culture of a country by drawing a map to show where the country is located.

Writing styles

You can make your book more fun by writing parts of it in different ways. This book is written mainly in **informational** style, which gives information to readers, but it also uses **instructional** text. Instructional text teaches the reader how to do something, such as write a book. **Narrative** text is written in story form. You could write a story about an experience you had with culture, such as playing a sport, being in a parade, painting a picture, or celebrating a birthday.

Write a narrative about the fun you had at your last birthday party. Include photographs.

Write a poem!

The poem below is about diversity. Write your own poem about how diversity makes your life interesting and fun.

My big Earth family

My big Earth family
is full of diversity,
bringing different cultures
to my community.
Learning about cultures is fun,
and teaches us to love everyone.

"Sensing" culture

Another text style is called **descriptive**. Descriptive text tells about a place, thing, or experience, using the senses of sight, hearing, smell, taste, and touch. Culture is all about the senses! The people on the opposite page are using their senses as they take part in different holiday customs.

Descriptive text

Using your senses, describe a special event you celebrated. Give examples of what you enjoyed the most and talk about all the fun you had.

- What did you see? Describe the colors and shapes of some costumes or other objects.
- What did you touch or feel?
- What sounds did you hear?
- What **aromas** did you smell?
- How did the foods you ate taste?

Mother's Day

*These children have blindfolded their mother so they can surprise her for Mother's Day. What can she **feel** on her skin? What does her sense of **smell** tell her about two of the gifts she will be receiving?*

Mardi Gras

*This boy is dancing in a Mardi Gras parade. What kind of music does he **hear** when he dances this way? Describe how his costume **looks**. What colors, shapes, and decorations does it have? What **sound** does the costume make when the boy moves?*

*This girl is carving a pumpkin for Halloween. She is removing the pumpkin's pulp and seeds. How does the pulp **feel** when she **touches** it?*

spices

Thanksgiving

*The girl below left is baking an apple pie for Thanksgiving dinner. What spices does she use? Describe how the pie will **smell** when it is baking and **taste** when it is done.*

apple pie

Halloween

Writing or typing?

You can write your book on the computer or by hand. There are different type styles you can use on a computer. If you are writing your book by hand, you can add color and try different ways of writing that look like words typed on a computer.

What is a font?

A **font** is a style of type. Different fonts are used throughout this book for different reasons. Most of the body of this book is written in a **plain text** font, which is easy to read. A **boldface**, or thick black, font is used to highlight words that may be new to readers. These words are explained on the page or defined in the glossary. The headings and subheadings are in larger type. A different font is used to make them stand out from the rest of the text. Headings can also be in color. Choose colors that match the pictures on the pages.

Captions and fact boxes

A **caption** gives you information about a picture. The captions in this book are written in *italics*. Letters in italics slant to the right. **Fact boxes** are separate from the main text to bring attention to special information, ask questions, or give instructions. They look like notebook pages, such as the one shown above right.

Type styles

- For your body text, choose a plain text font that is easy to read.
- Choose heading fonts that suit your subject.
- If you are writing your book by hand, use a thick pencil, pen, or marker to make words look like **boldface**.
- Write captions by *slanting* your words to look like an *italic* font.
- Make your headings larger and use colored pencils or markers.

Writing captions

Captions tell you what is going on in a picture. They may also ask you to use your imagination. Write captions for the pictures below. What is the boy on this pirate ship shouting? What might the children in the bottom picture be celebrating?

Font review

Plain text font is used to write most of the information in the book.

Boldface font is used to introduce new words.

Italic font is used for writing captions. A caption tells what is happening in a picture.

A different font can be used in fact boxes. Fact boxes give readers extra information or special directions.

Chapter headings are in large colored type.

Subheadings are smaller than chapter headings. They can also be in color.

Time to share!

Once you have written your **draft**, or first try at writing your book, it is time to read it to yourself. While reading, ask yourself these questions:

- How does my writing sound?
- Does it make sense?
- Have I included all the information I wanted to include?
- Have I written about my own observations or experiences with culture?
- Have I used different writing styles?
- Do my captions give interesting information? Do they describe what is happening in the pictures?
- Did I show how cultures are similar and different?
- Do my questions make my readers think?

*How can I **revise**, or rewrite, my book to make it better?*

Ask a parent or teacher to look at your work and help you organize and improve it.

Share your draft

- After you have read your draft and made some changes, it is time to share it with others.
- What questions did your classmates ask? Which parts did they feel needed to be changed?
- Other students can now take turns reading their drafts and asking for suggestions.
- Each person can then rewrite parts of their books that need to be changed.

A note from Bobbie

Don't worry about getting everything right. I revise my books many times before they are ready for my readers. Have fun writing and love what you write! Doing a book about culture is especially fun because it celebrates how creative we can be.

Editing and proofreading

After you have revised your writing, you may still find parts that you could have written more clearly. **Editing** is making sure that your writing is clear and correct. You may want to use some new words that are longer and more interesting than the ones you used. For example, you could use "demonstrate" instead of "show." **Proofreading** is checking for errors such as spelling mistakes, capital letters, **punctuation**, and sentence structure. After you have edited and proofread your book, ask others to do it, as well.

A ***thesaurus*** *gives* ***synonyms*** *for words. A synonym is a word that means the same as another word.*

Proofreading

- Are your sentences complete?
- Have you started names and the first word in each sentence with capital letters?
- Have you spelled names and other words correctly?
- Is your punctuation correct?

Editing checklist

- Have you covered all the information you intended to cover?
- Have you used the correct words? If you are not sure, look them up in a dictionary.
- Have you looked for new and interesting words in a thesaurus?
- Do your subheadings reflect the information in your paragraphs?
- Have you used different kinds of sentences?

Helpful questions

There are many questions in this book.

How do questions help you?

- They help you think more clearly.
- They help you review the work you have done and think about what you still need to cover.
- They help you think of other ideas to include in your book.
- Write some questions starting with the words who, what, where, when, and how.

"Who? What? Where? When? How? Can you tell us now?"

Designing your book

Designing is planning how your book will look so that people will want to read it. Writing text in a certain way, such as in fact boxes, is part of design. Using different fonts and colors also makes the book more attractive to readers.

Artwork and photographs

The other very important part of design is placing different kinds of pictures in your book. Pictures attract readers and make them interested in reading more. You can draw and paint your own pictures or take photographs of special holidays or events in your life. You can also download photos from the Internet. Ask a parent or teacher to help you find pictures that are free to use. Print these pictures and put them into your book. Look at the design of the spreads in this book to give you ideas about how to design your own book.

If you are painting your own pictures, photocopy them and place the copies into your book.

Your title page can contain one large picture, but you can add decorations or smaller pictures, as well.

Bobbie's tip

Before I start writing a book, I search for photos and artwork for each topic in my outline. Seeing the pictures helps me imagine how the book will look and how I will write each spread. Doing the cover first makes me feel excited about writing the book!

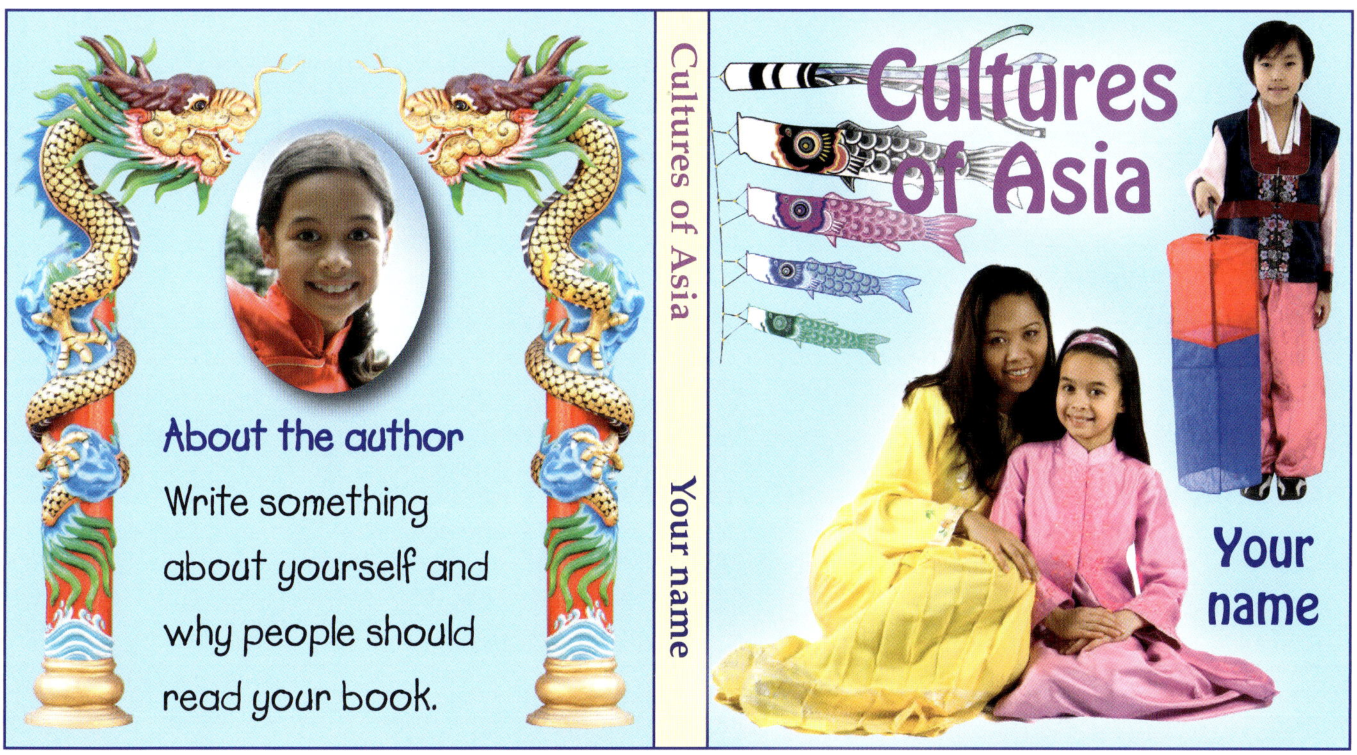

Above is an example of a front and back cover. You can do a book about your culture or the cultures of people who live in one country or on a single continent, such as Asia or North America. Draw your own cover pictures, borrow family photos, or use pictures you have downloaded from the Internet and cut out.

Celebrate your book!

Publishing your book is the last step. You will soon share your book with others in your classroom or library. If you wrote your book on the computer, you could make an eBook that many students could enjoy. Before you publish your book on the computer or by hand, you will need to complete all the parts of the book mentioned on pages 6 and 7—the copyright page, table of contents, glossary, and index. Find these pages in this book. They will help you create your own pages.

Binding your book

There are different ways to present your book to your readers. In some schools, the teacher or librarian has ways of **binding**, or tying, the pages of books together so other students can read them without losing pages. One of the easiest ways is to photocopy all your pages and then use a binder with plastic sleeves into which you will put your pages. These binders often have plastic pockets on the outside, as well, into which you can slip your front and back cover pictures.

Copyright page

Your copyright page will include the names of all the people who helped you with your book: parents, friends, teachers, as well as the sources of your art and photos. This page may also have a dedication. To whom will you dedicate your book?

Table of contents

Your table of contents is a list of the headings of all the spreads you wrote. The page numbers can be placed at the left or right of the headings. (See page 3.)

Glossary

Make a picture dictionary or word glossary and put it at the end of your book. Define special words about culture that your readers may not know. Sort the glossary in alphabetical order.

Index

The index is a list of the topics in this book. It is also in alphabetical order and gives the page numbers of where the topics can be found (see the index of this book on page 32).

Celebrate your book about culture! Dress in a costume, do a dance, or play some music. Culture is fun!

Do some funny artwork. Make people laugh.

Play some music. Do some dancing!

Have a carnival parade. Put on a play.

Glossary

Note: Some boldfaced words are defined where they appear in the book.

aroma A pleasant smell

binding Tying a book together at the spine

descriptive A writing style that uses the five senses of sight, hearing, smell, taste, and touch

editing Reading, checking facts, and revising parts of someone's writing

informational A writing style that gives information about something

instructional A writing style that gives instructions or directions on how to do something

narrative A writing style that tells something in story form

proofreading Checking a book for spelling, grammar, and punctuation

publisher A person or company that is responsible for printing and distributing a written book, magazine, or newspaper

punctuation The use of marks, such as periods or commas, to make the meaning of a sentence clear

Index

big ideas 12
binding 30
body of book 18–19, 22
captions 22, 23, 24
copyright page 7, 30
cover 6, 29
design 28–29
editing 26
fact boxes 22, 23, 28
fonts 22–23, 28
glossary 7, 8, 22, 30, 31
headings 18, 22, 23, 30
index 7, 30, 31
outlines 15, 29
pictures/art 5, 6, 7, 8, 9, 10, 12, 13, 15, 17, 19, 22, 23, 28, 29, 30, 31
proofreading 26
publishing 4, 30
questions 14, 22, 24, 25, 27
research 16–17
spreads 18, 19, 28, 29, 30
subheadings 18, 22, 23, 26
table of contents 7, 15, 30
title page 7, 29
writer's notebook 9, 14
writing styles 19, 20–21, 24

Further reading

Celebrations in My World series

Native Nations of North America series

Cultural Traditions in My World series

Spotlight on my Country series

Lands, Peoples, and Cultures serie